TO THE TEACHER

Pendulum Press is proud to offer the NOW AGE ILLUSTRATED Series to schools throughout the country. This completely new series has been prepared by the finest artists and illustrators from around the world. The script adaptations have been prepared by professional writers and revised by qualified reading consultants.

Implicit in the development of the Series are several assumptions. Within the limits of propriety, anything a child reads and/or wants to read is *per se* an educational tool. Educators have long recognized this and have clamored for materials that incorporate this premise. The sustained popularity of the illustrated format, for example, has been documented, but it has not been fully utilized for educational purposes. Out of this realization, the NOW AGE ILLUSTRATED Series evolved.

In the actual reading process, the illustrated panel encourages and supports the student's desire to read printed words. The combination of words and picture helps the student to a greater understanding of the subject; and understanding, that comes from reading, creates the desire for more reading.

The final assumption is that reading as an end in itself is self-defeating. Children are motivated to read material that satisfies their quest for knowledge and understanding of their world. In this series, they are exposed to some of the greatest stories, authors, and characters in the English language. The Series will stimulate their desire to read the original edition when their reading skills are sufficiently developed. More importantly, reading books in the NOW AGE ILLUSTRATED Series will help students establish a mental "pegboard" of information — images, names, and concepts — to which they are exposed. Let's assume, for example, that a child sees a television commercial which features Huck Finn in some way. If he has read the NOW AGE Huck Finn, the TV reference has meaning for him which gives the child a surge of satisfaction and accomplishment.

After using the NOW AGE ILLUSTRATED editions, we know that you will share our enthusiasm about the series and its concept.

—The Editors

ABOUT THE AUTHOR

Robert Louis Stevenson was born in Edinburgh, Scotland in 1850. An industrious person, he carried two books with him always: one to read and one in which to write.

His imagination for a story was sparked often by simple clues. *Treasure Island,* for example, was reputedly inspired by a treasure map and a. twelve-year-old boy. Many of the adventures are similar to ones Stevenson experienced as a child.

Stevenson was interested not only in buried treasure, pirates, and sea adventure, but also in human psychology. His fascination with the conflict of good and evil in man prompted him to write *Dr. Jekyll and Mr. Hyde.* Partially because of his Calvinist upbringing, he thought that man was always suppressing his evil nature. This nature, so long held back, breaks loose violently in the character of Mr. Hyde.

Stevenson was a collector of ideas. Often he borrowed expressions or thoughts from other writers, but his own style was unmistakable. He traveled extensively, married an American, and retreated for health reasons to the South Sea islands. There, in 1894, he died of tuberculosis, but not until he had established himself as the "tusitala" or "the teller of tales" to the natives.

R.L. Stevenson Treasure Island

Adapted by
JOHN NORWOOD FAGO

Illustrated by
NARDO CRUZ

a

VINCENT FAGO
production

Long John
Silver

Squire
Trelawney

Jim Hawkins

Billy Bones

Dr. Livesey

Squire Trelawney, Dr. Livesey, and the rest having asked me to write down the whole of the particulars about Treasure Island, I, Jim Hawkins, take up my pen in the year of our Grace 17.... and go back to the time when my father kept the "Admiral Benbow" Inn . . . .

Fifteen men on a dead man's chest. Yo-ho-ho, and a bottle of rum.

FOREMAST HILL

NORTH INLET

SPYGLASS HILL

MIZZENMAST HILL

SKELETON ISLAND

ADMIRAL BENBOW

I'll never forget the day Billy Bones came into my life. He arrived at my father's inn and asked for a glass of rum.

And so he came to stay.

This is a pleasant spot with a nice view of the sea, sir. Do you get many people coming to stay?

No, sir. I'm sorry to say. It's very quiet here.

Bring in my chest. I'll stay awhile and trouble you little for I'm a plain man. I just like to look at the sea.

He was a quiet man, and we could see he did not want to run in to other sailors.

One day he pulled me aside and said. . . .

Here is some gold. Just let me know when I owe you more.

You, Jim, keep watch for a sailor with one leg. Do your job well and I'll pay you for it.

Yes, sir.

He stayed month after month but only talked to people when he was drunk. One night when Dr. Livesey had come to see my father, who was ill, Bones started. . . .

Quiet over there!

You keep on drinking that rum and you'll end up killing yourself.

Bones got mad and came at the Doctor with a knife.

Put that knife away this minute or I'll have you hanged.

For a minute we thought there'd be trouble, but Bones gave in.

A few days later Bones was surprised by an unexpected guest. . . .

Ah Bill, I haven't seen you in years.

So you finally found me, Black Dog. Well. . .what do you want?

I want a glass of rum. Then we'll sit and talk like old shipmates.

They talked quietly for a while. All of a sudden they began to shout and Black Dog took off running.

The captain staggered inside and fell on the floor. Just then Dr. Livesey stopped to see my father.

What shall we do?

I warned him. He's had a heart attack just as I said he would. Get me a pan.

I'll bleed* him just enough to keep him quiet.

When I stopped in to see him later, he was weak but worried.

Jim, it's my sea chest they'll want if they kill me. You tell the doctor to get everyone up here when they come.

They can take care of Flint's crew. I was Old Flint's first mate and the only one who knows his secret. But don't you tell anyone what I've said unless they put the Black Spot on me or you see a sailor with one leg. You hear, Jim?

* to let blood flow from the body for medical reasons.

That night my father died and I didn't think of anything else until the next morning.

I'm blind. Will anybody tell me where I am.

At the Admiral Benbow Inn, sir.

He asked to be taken inside but when I held out my arm. . . .

Take me right to Captain Bones or I'll break your arm.

He gave a note to Bones and then left quickly.

Six hours to go. I'll make it yet.

UNTIL 10

But as Bones stood up, he grabbed his throat and fell to the floor—dead!

Mother!

UNTIL 10

I told my mother all I knew and we tried to get some help. No one would do anything except ride to find the doctor.

If no one will help us then we'll go back alone. Come, Jim.

We went through Bones' sea chest and my mother took what money he owed her.

I am an honest woman. I'll take only what is mine.

Suddenly we heard a strange whistle coming from the hill outside.

Come, Jim, I have what I need.

I'll take this too, just to be sure.

The pirates went right to the inn and were ordered to go in and search.

Pew, someone beat us to it. They've gone through the sea chest.

It's that boy! I wish I'd put out his eyes. Go, men, and find him.

A moment later the strange whistle sounded again. I had thought that it was the pirates signal to attack, but it seemed to fill them with fear.

There's Dirk again. We have to go, men.

You're so close to getting thousands of dollars and you're going to leave?

Don't stand there talking, Pew. Let's go!

*His friends left without him, and Pew ran on. . .
to his death.*

*After a useless chase, the riders
who were government men
sent by the doctor, came back
to the inn.*

What were they
after?

I think I have it in my
pocket. I'd like to put
it in a safe place.

You're right, son. Dogger,
put the boy on the horse
with you and we'll go
report to Dr. Livesey.

Dr. Livesey was having dinner with Squire Trelawney.

Officer Danse told them what had happened, and the two men were very surprised and interested.

Come in, Mr. Danse.

Good evening, friend Jim. What brings you here?

Mr. Danse, you're a good man.

I'll keep Hawkins here and give him some dinner.

While I ate a big dinner Mr. Danse and the men talked. Finally Danse left.

And now, Livesey. . . .

You've heard of this Flint, haven't you?

The evil Flint was well-known to the Squire as was the fact that he had buried treasure.

If there is a clue to his treasure here, I'll rent a ship. We'll find the treasure if it takes a year.

We'll open these papers if Jim says we can.

I said yes and the doctor opened the seals to the papers with great care. A map of an island fell out, with latitude and longitude, soundings, and names of hills, bays, and inlets—all that would be needed to bring a ship safely to the island.

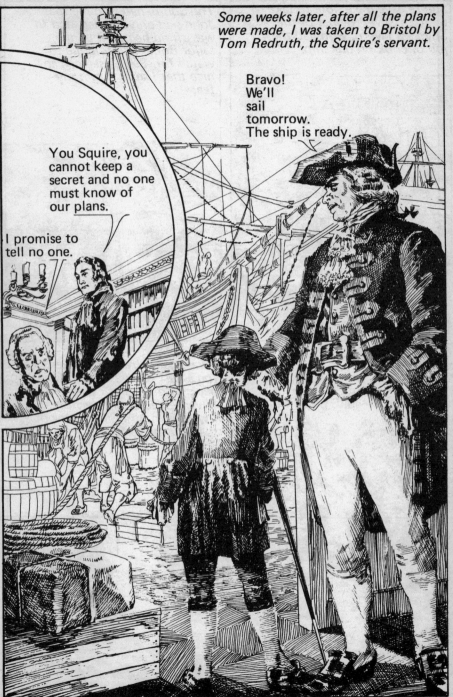

Squire gave me a note to take to John Silver, owner of the Spyglass tavern, who had the job of cook on our ship.

The Squire had told me that John had only one leg, and I was afraid he might be the sailor Bones had told me to watch for. But he seemed so nice that I soon forgot my fear.

All of a sudden a sailor saw me and ran.

Stop him! That's Black Dog!

Run and get him, Harry. He didn't pay his bill. Black what?

I was again afraid but Silver was too smart for me. Harry came back without Black Dog and Silver yelled at him terribly. So I was again sure Silver was not a man for me to fear.

I'll go with you to the Captain. This is important business, and he must know about it.

That afternoon we all went aboard the Hispaniola, our ship, to give her a final check.

Show him in.

Captain Smollett is here, sir. He wants to speak with you.

I don't like this trip. I don't like the men and I don't like my officer. That's what I've come to tell you.

Maybe you don't like the men who hired you either.

Stay awhile. You have said too much and too little, Captain. You don't like this trip. Tell me why?

I hear you have a map of an island where treasure is buried. This island is located. . . .

I never told a soul.

Everyone on this ship knows about it, sir. This trip could end in the death of everyone of us!

He gave the exact location.

Do you fear a mutiny?

To protect this ship we must make new plans. You must do what I ask or I shall quit.

The Squire was angry about the changes but they were made. Just before sunrise the next day we set sail.

Ours was a fine ship with a good crew and a captain who knew his business. Our trip to Treasure Island was a good one.

Long John was obeyed by everyone in the crew. He always seemed glad to see me when I came into his galley* which was very neat.

Come in, Jim, and I'll tell you a story or two. This is my parrot, Captain Flint, who was just telling me we're in for a good trip.

Pieces of eight. Pieces of eight.

The captain said he must have been wrong about the crew for they worked very hard. . .and he learned to love the ship.

She's sailing well, sir, but we're not there yet.

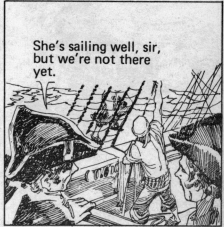

The Squire tried to keep the men happy. He kept a barrel of apples on the deck and let the men help themselves whenever they wanted, and he gave them extra rum.

You're spoiling the men. They will get lazy.

But good did come of the apple barrel. One night I climbed in to find an apple and almost fell asleep there when a heavy man came up and sat down against it.

* a kitchen

Silver told of how he was an officer on Flint's ship and of how he lost his leg and Pew lost his eyes.

It wasn't long before I knew that our lives would depend on what I heard.

Yes, I've seen Flint's ship covered with blood and ready to sink because of all the gold she was carrying.

Flint was a good pirate. The best!

Most of the men on board were Flint's and they were glad to be here. Flint was afraid of me and the men know it. They trust me, mate, and you can, too.

I didn't like this job until I had this little talk with you. But I like it now. Let's shake hands on it.

Then Silver gave a low whistle and a third man joined them.

How long are we going to wait? I want to get at their wine.

As long as I can. The Captain is sailing the ship for us. The Doctor and the Squire will find the treasure and help us get it on board. I say we'll wait until I think the time is right! Get me an apple, Dirk.

You can guess how afraid I was....

Forget that. Let's go get some rum.

Dirk, thank God, went to get a cup instead.

Just then I heard a cry....

None of the other Doctor's men want to join us.

Land Ho!

Everyone rushed to the deck, and I climbed out of the barrel.

Doctor, get the Captain and Squire to the cabin. I must tell you all some news.

When they were all there, I told them what I had heard.

That Silver is something.

Captain, you were right. I will follow your orders.

I think we should plan carefully and try to take them by surprise.

You can count on my men and myself.

That is three plus ourselves. I wonder if any of the crew will help us. We'll have to find out as soon as we can.

And so it looked like our six grown men against nineteen of them.

We anchored the next morning and knew the mutiny might happen any minute.

If I give another order I think the crew will attack. We had better let one man handle them.

Who is that?

Silver, sir. He wants to keep things quiet, too. Let the men go ashore and Silver will bring them back quiet as lambs.

It's a hot day men. If anyone wants to go ashore he may do so for the afternoon.

After saying this the Captain left and Silver took charge. It was plain to the crew that Silver was their captain now.

For some crazy reason I decided to go ashore with the men so I hid in one of the smaller boats.

Jim is that you? Keep your head down.

Jim! Jim!

I ran until I thought I would drop.

I enjoyed exploring the island until I heard two people talking close by.

I tried to get closer so I could hear.

At last I could see as well.

I'm giving you a chance to join us. Now make up your mind.

I'd rather lose a hand than join you.

I'd found an honest man who would join our side but a horrible scream made me forget for a minute.

In God's name what was that?

I guess that was poor Allen.

At this Tom jumped forward.

God rest his soul. Kill me too if you can catch me.

And Tom took off for the beach but he did not get very far.

Silver was on top of him in a moment and stabbed him twice with his knife. For the next few minutes my head felt like it was going around in circles.

When my head cleared I ran faster than I had ever run before, until. . . .

What's that? A monkey or a bear?

Whatever it was ran off like a deer making a wide circle. . . .

Not knowing what the thing was I thought I would have been better off staying with Long John.

Who are you?

Ben Gunn and I haven't spoken to a human in three years.

Many a night I've dreamed of cheese.

If I ever get back to my ship you shall have some.

But how am I to get back to my ship?

Not you, I know.

I told him the whole story. . . .

You just trust old Ben Gunn.

He told me how he'd been on Flint's ship, The Walrus, when Flint came to the island and buried the treasure and how when on another ship he'd begged the captain to stop and search for it. But when after twelve days they hadn't found it, they left Ben with just a gun and a shovel and sailed off. He had lived on berries, goat's meat and fish and had found the treasure which he would share with those who safely took him home.

But how am I to get back to my ship?

Well, I have a little boat just under that white rock. . . .

Just then we heard the sound of a cannon.

They've started to fight. Follow me!

We ran toward the ship until suddenly. . . .

It seems that just after I left the ship the Doctor and Mr. Hunter came ashore too to have a look at Flint's old fort. Some happenings I knew nothing about led to what we now saw. Let me go back then and tell you about it.

The Doctor left Hunter to guard the small boat and had gone on alone.

We have wine on board but we could use some fresh water.

He then heard the same cry I had heard of poor Allen being killed.

My God. I hope that isn't Jim.

We haven't a moment to lose.

Gray almost fainted when he heard the scream. He's scared. I think he'll join us.

We decided to fight from the fort. The Doctor with Hunter and Joyce took food and guns to the fort while the Captain and Squire stayed on board to guard the ship.

If any man causes any trouble, I'll shoot him dead.

Leaving Hunter and Joyce to guard the fort, the Doctor returned to the others on the boat.

Gray joined them, and the boat headed for shore.

Gray, I order you to follow your captain.

Suddenly they saw that the cannon on deck was being loaded.

Israel Hands was Flint's best gunner.

Mr. Trelawney, shoot Mr. Hands you are able.

But just as Squire fired, Hands ducked, and another man fell.

They'll have to run fast!

They're only taking one boat. The rest are coming by shore to cut us off.

They were just a few feet from shore when a cannonball fell near them and flooded the boat.

Watch it men. The boat is sinking.

They waded to shore as fast as they could and headed for the fort. Just as they got over the wall seven mutineers showed up.

Good work men. It looks like one of them is dead.

One man was dead, and the others ran. But a few seconds later a gun sounded from the bushes.

They got Tom.

Tom was dying and asked for a prayer. . . .

Please, sir, a prayer.

. . . .without another word, he died.

Back to my story, then. . .I asked Ben Gunn to come to the fort, but he wanted to be sure the Squire would share the treasure with him.

And when they want to see Ben Gunn, you can find him where you found him today.

The pirates began firing from the ship and so it was several hours before I made my return. They were all glad to see me.

I told my story and found out from the Doctor that Ben's strangeness was not unusual.

I think he might be crazy.

No, I think he's all right.

I happen to carry cheese in my tobacco box. You take it to Ben Gunn.

He wanted cheese did he?

Yes, sir, cheese!

Before supper we buried old Tom.

After we ate, we talked about our plans.

There were nineteen of them, but two are gone.

We'll keep after them until we've won or they run away with the Hispaniola.

It will be the first ship I've ever lost.

With luck, too much rum or malaria* will take care of them within the week.

* a sickness caught in hot countries

I slept very well that night but woke up early.

They've put up a flag of truce*.

* peace

Watch out, men! This could be a trick.

It's Captain Silver. I've come to talk.

Captain Silver. . . who is he?

Me, sir. The men made me Captain after you left. Let me come and talk to you.

You'd better sit down.

It's a cold day to sit on the sand.

As my cook I treated you well, as a mutineer you will hang!

Well now we'll give you a choice. Give us the map and let us get the treasure. Once we have it safely on board we will let you come, too. We'll drop you somewhere with food and tell the first ship we see to come after you.

Now listen to me. You send your men up here one by one without their guns and I'll take you all to England for a fair trial. These are my last words about it. Either you do as I say or I'll shoot you the next time we meet.

Help me up.

Not I!

Laugh at me, will you. Before the hour's gone I'll give you something to laugh at. Those that die will be the lucky ones!

I gave Silver my final words on the subject. Soon we should know what will happen.

The Captain told us his plan and after getting things ready, we waited.

Suddenly the fighting began.

All hands to the battle.

In the first few minutes two were killed, one ran, but four came right at us.

Hunter. . .watch out!

Fight them out in the open men. Use your swords.

Go around the house, men, around the house.

Poor Hunter was knocked out with his own gun.

In a few seconds all that was left of the pirates were the five who had died.

We saw right away what the battle had cost us.

But five of them are dead.

We have better odds than we started with.

Later that afternoon the Doctor went to find Ben Gunn and I took off to find Ben's boat.

It was dark by the time I found it so I planned to paddle out to the Hispaniola, cut her ropes and let her float where she may.

I did this easily but got carried along with the current.

I'm drifting toward the open sea.

I began to pray thinking I was lost for good. I fell asleep and dreamed.

To my surprise I woke up still alive—not in the open sea, but somewhere on the other side of the island.

I just floated along for a while until I saw the Hispaniola with nobody on deck steering her.

Those pirates must have left or be as drunk as can be.

I thought I might be able to sail her back to the Captain.

I got aboard but a wave sank my little boat and I had no way to escape.

I found one pirate dead and Israel Hands drunk and hurt.

Brandy, get me some brandy.

Are you all right, Mr. Hands?

Looking around I found a bottle for Hands and some food for me.

I'd better hurry.

I am your Captain until you're told otherwise, Mr. Hands.

You can't sail this ship but if you give me food and take care of my wounds, I'll help you.

I told him I would do as he asked, and in a few minutes we were headed for the North Inlet. I was pleased and proud but frightened, too.

Get me a bottle of wine, Jim. This brandy is too strong.

I couldn't believe anything was too strong for him, so. . . .

I watched to see what he would do. . . .

He took a knife from his dead mate and I knew I had to be more careful.

Maybe I'll make it without trouble.

It was difficult sailing but with Hands' help it went smoothly until. . . .

I jumped aside and the wheel spun out of control.

No you don't, Mr Hands.

Stay where you are.

But my guns were wet and needed to be reloaded.

Suddenly the ship hit ground.

I climbed the ropes and reloaded my guns.

Stay where you are, Hands, or I'll shoot to kill.

His knife sailed up and pinned me to the mast just as both guns went off.

Hands fell into the sea and after freeing myself, I cut the sails to keep her pretty still and started ashore.

Now to get back to the fort.

At last I came to the clearing.

There doesn't seem to be anyone here.

I knew something was wrong when I heard. . . .

Pieces of eight! Pieces of eight!

At the sound of Silver's parrot I turned and ran into a pair of arms that closed about me and held me.

Who's there? Bring a torch, Dirk.

So, it's Jim Hawkins. I find that interesting.

I want to know where my friends are and what's been going on.

Yesterday the Doctor came and told me the ship was gone. Said my men sold out— gave me some food and left. Don't know where they are.

I have something to tell you too. . . .

I was excited and told how I had heard their plans while hiding in the apple barrel and then how I cut the ship loose so they'd never find her.

Let me live and I'll save you from hanging. Kill me and you'll be in even more trouble.

Kill you I will.

I'm Captain here! You'll do as I say.

I've had enough listening to you, Silver.

You who wants to see who's captain, take out your sword. I'll see the color of your blood.

No one moved but my heart pounded so I thought I would explode.

Listen, Silver, I want to meet with the other men. It's my right.

The rules say we can.

Yes, a meeting.

When I looked in the bay and saw the ship was gone, I gave up. But I'd save your life if you keep me from hanging.

It's a bargain then. Now tell me why the Doctor gave me the treasure map.

I must have looked so surprised that he asked me no more questions.

That look means nothing. I wonder if it's good or bad.

After some time. . . .

Here they come.

Let them come. I'll take care of them.

Step up, men, I won't eat you.

The Black Spot! Why isn't this lucky. You've cut it out of the Bible.

Stop all the talk, Silver, just turn it over and read it.

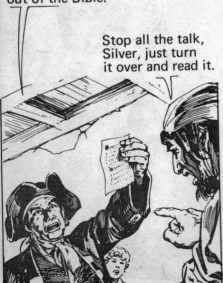

The Black Spot was a way of telling Silver he was no longer Captain.

No longer Captain, huh? You write pretty but I'm still Captain until I hear what's wrong and give my answers.

We all agreed. You made a mess of the trip, let the others get away, and now there's this boy.

You're crazy, the whole bunch of you! You all know what I wanted. If you'd done it, we'd be on board the Hispaniola tonight with the treasure. Pirates! You'd make better farmers. That boy is our last chance. They want him too. And as to why I let them go, look here!

You lost the ship, I found the treasure. Pick another Captain if you want. I'm finished talking to the likes of you.

That was the end of that.

We were awakened in the morning by a loud voice.

Jim it is.

Well let me take care of your men first. Then we'll talk about Jim.

The men took the medicine he gave them more like babies than like pirates.

Well that takes care of everyone. Now I'd like to talk about the boy.

—No!—

Silver took over.

Si-lence! Doctor, I want to thank you for what you've done. I will let you speak to the boy if he promises not to run away.

I promised so. . . .

Then, Doctor, if you'll step outside. I'll bring the boy out, and he can tell you his story.

Silver kept the men in order with looks that would kill.

Go slow, son. They might come after us if we seem to be in a hurry.

The boy will tell you I saved his life. I ask you to save mine.

Why, John, you're not afraid are you?

I'm not afraid but I don't want to hang either. You won't forget the bad or the good I've done, I know. So I'll leave you alone to talk with the boy. Remember, no one wants to hang.

Come on, Jim. Climb the fence and we'll run for it.

You wouldn't do that and neither will I. I gave my word and so I stay. But listen. . . .

The ship! My boy, every step of the way it's you who has saved lives.

I told him what I had done with the ship.

I want this boy kept safe, do you hear. Yell if you need help. Watch out for trouble if you find the treasure. Keep Jim safe and if we get out of here I'll do my best to save you.

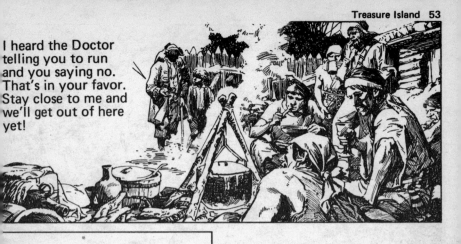

I heard the Doctor telling you to run and you saying no. That's in your favor. Stay close to me and we'll get out of here yet!

They have the ship but once we get the treasure we'll have the upper hand.

As he talked he built up their hopes and his own as well, I'm sure.

As for the boy, why, once we've got the treasure we'll give Mr. Hawkins his share for all his help.

Silver was careful to let me know he'd try to keep me safe and keep himself from hanging.

And so we went to look for the treasure.

Following the maps, we headed for the area between Spyglass and Mizzenmast Hill.

Hey, yo-ho!

This is a good piece of canvas.

There's something strange about the way these bones are lying.

Just looking told us the bones had been placed in a special way.

This is Flint's joke for sure. He killed all six of his men when he buried his treasure. Six men. . .there are six of us too.

The body lay exactly on the spot of the map we were looking for.

If ever a spirit would walk after death, it would be Flint's. He died bad.

He'd always sing "Fifteen Men" when he was getting drunk.

Stop that talking! Let's move in for the gold.

The men kept close together frightened by the talk of spirits. All of a sudden a voice came through the trees.

It's Flint!

Don't be silly. It's a voice I know but I can't think of who. . . .

They were his last words.

But Silver would not be fooled.

I'll not be beaten by man or spirit. I was never afraid of Flint and I'm not afraid now!

Watch out, John. Don't cross a spirit.

Spirit? But there was an echo. Who ever heard of a spirit with an echo or a shadow?

*The men seemed less
afraid now.*

By God! It
seemed like
Ben Gunn.

It was like Flint's voice
but like somebody else's
too. It was like. . . .

But Ben Gunn is just
as dead as Flint.

True, but nobody minds
Ben Gunn dead or alive.

And so we went on until. . . .

*We found the hiding place and saw
that the treasure had been taken.*

im, stand here.

Giving me a gun?
So you're changing
sides again.

Two gold coins! So you're
the one who is never
wrong.

Dig away, boys.
You'll find more
for sure.

Just then three shots rang out in the woods above us.

It seemed that Ben Gunn had foun the treasure years before and hid it in his cave. When Dr. Livesey had discovered this he traded the map for the chance of getting to Ben's cave where he could be safe, have plenty of food, and help to guard the treasure.

We figured you'd be in trouble so we sent Ben out to scare you and give us time to get here and help.

If I didn't have Jim you'd have let them cut me to pieces.

That's right, John.

e destroyed one of the boats
d set out in the other to
tch the Hispaniola.

Everything was fine on board.

Lucky for us she's
still here.

Take us to shore and then
come back and stand guard
until morning.

e went to Ben's cave.

Thank you
for your
help, sir.

John Silver,
I told you I
would help you
and I will, but
all those men
died because
of you. But a
promise is a
promise.

ou're a good boy, Jim.
ut I don't think we'll
il together again. You
d many narrow escapes
r me.

at terrible trouble had come with this treasure.

We went to work in the morning and it took us three days to get the treasure on board.

The ship loaded, we held a meeting and decided, to the great joy of Ben Gunn, to leave the three mutineers on the island with food and supplies. Then we set sail for the nearest port to hire new men for the long trip home.

We went ashore as soon as we arrived.

It's good to see so many smiling faces again.

But when we returned to the ship. . . .

Silver's gone with a bag of our gold.

we were glad to be rid of him at last.

To make a long story short, we had a good trip home and each of us got our share of the treasure to use as we liked. We never heard of John Silver again but I'm sure he's living happily somewhere. He'd better live happily in this world for he has a poor chance at such a life in the next world.

The End

WORDS TO KNOW

inn	pirates
mutiny	shipmates

QUESTIONS

1. How does Jim Hawkins come to be the owner of a treasure map?

2. To whom did the treasure map first belong?

3. How did the story of the treasure map "get out" to all the men on board the ship?

4. When did Jim first suspect that Long John Silver was a pirate?

5. Why did Ben Gunn act so strange when he first saw young Jim Hawkins?

6. What are mutineers?

7. Why did Dr. Livesey give the treasure map to Long John Silver without any fight?

8. What happenings in the story show us how brave Jim Hawkins was?

9. Explain why you think Long John Silver was a good or evil man.